Julius Caesar

Sweet Cherry

Publishing

Published by Sweet Cherry Publishing Limited
Unit E, Vulcan Business Complex,
Vulcan Road,
Leicester, LE5 3EB,
United Kingdom

First published in the USA in 2013
ISBN: 978-1-78226-071-4

©Macaw Books

Title: Julius Caesar
North American Edition

All rights reserved. No part of this publication may be
reproduced or utilized in any form or by any means, electronic
or mechanical, including photocopying, recording, or using
any information storage and retrieval system, without prior
permission in writing from the publisher.

Text & Illustration by Macaw Books 2013

www.sweetcherrypublishing.com

Printed and bound by Wai Man Book Binding (China) Ltd. Kowloon, H.K.

~ About ~
Shakespeare

William Shakespeare, regarded as the greatest writer in the English language, was born in Stratford-upon-Avon in Warwickshire, England (around April 23, 1564). He was the third of eight children born to John and Mary Shakespeare.

Shakespeare was a poet, playwright, and dramatist. He is often known as England's national poet and the "Bard of Avon." Thirty-eight plays, 154 sonnets, two long narrative poems, and several other poems are attributed to him. Shakespeare's plays have been translated into every major existent language and are performed more often than those of any other playwright.

Julius Caesar: Julius Caesar is one of the members of the Roman senate. He has come back to Rome after a victory. He refuses the crown three times, but he wants to be a Roman ruler. Though he is killed early on in the play, every character is preoccupied with him.

Octavius Caesar: He is the nephew of Julius Caesar. He succeeds Julius Caesar as Rome's monarch, ending the republic in Rome. He is an authoritative figure like Julius. He joins Mark Antony to fight the conspirators, Brutus and Cassius.

Mark Antony: He is a loyal friend of Julius Caesar. He is spontaneous, clever, passionate, and lives in the  moment. He is resourceful and proves to be a dangerous enemy to Brutus and Cassius.

Brutus: Brutus is one of the conspirators. He is a high-ranking nobleman and easily influenced. He conspired to kill Julius because Julius was getting too powerful and posed a threat to the republic. He puts the good of Rome before his personal feelings.

Julius Caesar

The citizens of Rome had gathered in the streets to greet Julius Caesar, who was returning in triumph having defeated and killed the sons

of Pompey, another Roman
senator he had killed previously.

As the public gathered
round Caesar, a soothsayer called
out a warning to him. "Beware
of the Ides (March 15)!"

"He is only a dreamer,"
said Caesar, and passed by.

In those times, a king or dictator did not rule Rome. It was a democracy and was ruled by senators—powerful and wise men forming an assembly called the senate. Roman citizens were very proud of this, which is why some of them were also worried that Julius Caesar was becoming more powerful than the other senators. Would he stop being a senator and become king or emperor? Would Rome stop being a democracy?

"Caesar, I offer you the crown," said Mark Antony to Senator Julius Caesar. Caesar pushed the crown away. Thrice

the crown was offered to him and thrice he refused it. The third time, when Caesar reached the marketplace, the people cheered so loudly that he felt hurt that they were glad he had refused.

Senator Cassius noticed this and became doubtful of Caesar's

intentions. As Caesar rode into
Rome, Cassius talked to Senator

Brutus about his concerns. Caesar was very attached to Brutus, and Brutus to him. But that did not mean Brutus wanted Caesar, or anybody else for that matter, to become king or emperor. Brutus believed in democracy, and hated the idea of Caesar robbing Roman citizens of their democratic rights, individual freedom, and dignity.

Senator Casca was passing by and also joined in the discussion. "We are Caesar's equals. Caesar should not be allowed

to lord over us," Cassius urged
Brutus. "I will think about it,"
said Brutus, concern in his voice.

Cassius saw that Brutus was
noble but could be influenced,
and then Caesar's position
really would be threatened. He
wrote some letters in different

handwriting, as if they were from different people. They all said that Caesar was becoming too ambitious and wanted Brutus to do something about it. Cassius's plan was to put these letters in Brutus's room for him to find.

That night there was a storm.
Casca was out in the bad weather
and felt strange and terrible
things happening—as though
the gods in heaven were at war.
He met an elderly senator named
Cicero, who told him that he had
already arranged a meeting of
some important Roman noblemen

who also thought that Caesar
should not be allowed to become
a tyrant. Another senator named
Cinna also joined them and
was given the task of placing
the letters in Brutus's room.

Brutus could not get to sleep
that night, thinking about what
Cassius had said: "Personally

I have nothing against Caesar, but there is every chance of him accepting the crown next time it is offered and becoming King of Rome. We must prevent that. We must think of him as a serpent's egg and kill him while he is still in the shell."

His servant-boy, Lucius, then brought him the letters that had been placed in his room. As he read them, Brutus became more concerned. He also remembered that the very next day was the Ides or 15th of

March, when something terrible
had been predicted for Caesar.

Cassius and others who had
formed a group against Caesar
entered with their faces covered.
"Give me your hands, all of you,"
said Brutus. The conspiracy or
plot was made to kill Caesar the
very next day when he attended a

meeting with other senators at the Senate House. Cassius suggested that Mark Antony should also be killed, as he was too close to Caesar and too clever, but Brutus did not agree to this. However, what if Caesar, already warned by the soothsayer, decided not to come to the senate? The conspirators

decided that if this happened,
they would go to his house
and fetch him themselves.

By the time the conspirators
were gone, it was early morning.
Brutus's wife, Portia, was worried.
Who were those men who had
come hiding their faces? What

was making her husband look so troubled? Brutus was able to avoid her questions only because there happened to be another senator visiting him at that time.

At Caesar's palace, his wife Calpurnia was trying her best to stop him from going outdoors, as

she had had a dream in which she had seen a lioness walking about in the marketplace, clouds raining blood, and other strange visions. "Cowards die many times before their death," declared Caesar.

"The valiant never taste of death but once." Calpurnia still pleaded that Caesar should send Mark Antony to tell the senate he was sick.

Caesar was about to agree when Decius, one of the conspirators, arrived. Decius made Caesar feel that the senators would think him cowardly and foolish if he did not turn up at the senate simply because Calpurnia had had a bad dream. Other conspirators

arrived soon after—Publius,
Brutus, Casca, Ligarius, Cinna,

Metellus, and Trebonius. Caesar was a little surprised that they had come to fetch him, but pleasantly so. He got ready at once, saying, "I do not want to keep the senate waiting."

A citizen had learned of the plot to kill Caesar and tried to alert him as he passed by, but Caesar paid no attention to him. To the soothsayer who stood by the road, he called out lightly, "The Ides of March has come!"

"Ay, Caesar. But not gone," replied the soothsayer gravely.

At Brutus's house, Portia was getting nervous and kept sending Lucius to the marketplace to find out what was happening.

As Caesar went up the stairs of the senate, the conspirators tactfully removed Mark Antony from Caesar's side and

surrounded him. They insisted
that Caesar sign a petition
and, on that pretext, got closer
and closer to him. Caesar
refused to sign, and to keep
him focused on the petition,
Brutus knelt down before him.
Meanwhile, the conspirators
were ready to attack.

Casca struck the first blow, stabbing Caesar in the neck from behind. Then the others fell upon him. Caught completely off-guard, Caesar stood his ground, trying to ward off the blows with his hands. But as Brutus also stabbed him, he cried

out, "You too, Brutus!" Then he
fell down dead, where a statue
of his old rival, Pompey, stood.

"Liberty! Freedom! Tyranny is
dead!" cried the conspirators. They
bathed their hands in Caesar's
blood and waved their swords
in triumph. A shocked Antony

returned to his house. Soon, he
sent a message saying that he
wanted to come back, but only if
Brutus assured him of his safety.

Brutus gave him that
assurance, and Antony returned.
He cleverly persuaded Brutus and
the other conspirators to allow

him to make a public speech at Caesar's funeral. Cassius, who had masterminded the plot, did not like the idea at all. But Brutus told him that Caesar should have all the funeral rites that he deserved. And so that Antony could not sway the public, Brutus decided to speak first and make it clear that Antony was speaking only by their permission.

The citizens of Rome panicked at first, but then they went to the marketplace, demanding an explanation. Brutus asked some of them to listen to him, while others listened to Cassius on another street.

"This is my explanation," said Brutus. "I loved Caesar, but I loved Rome more. Caesar was a threat to Rome's democracy and so he was killed. There are tears for his love, joy for his fortune, honor for his valor, and death for his ambition."

The people were quite
satisfied with Brutus's explanation.

Mark Antony brought
Caesar's body out of the senate
to the marketplace. Brutus left,
asking the citizens to listen
to Antony's funeral speech.

"Friends, Romans, countrymen,
lend me your ears," began Antony.
"I have come to bury Caesar, not

praise him." But very cleverly, Antony soon began to praise Caesar, reminding the people that Caesar's conquests had gone into the public treasury, not his own. He had felt for the poor, and as for ambition, he had refused the

crown when it had been offered to him. "Yet Brutus says he was ambitious, and he is an honorable man," he added sarcastically.

Upon hearing this, the citizens felt that there was much truth in what Mark Antony was saying. Antony broke down many times during the course of his

speech. "Judgment has been given to brutish beasts, and men have lost their reason," he wept. This was actually an appeal to people's emotions rather than their reason. The people began to feel that Brutus, Cassius, and the other conspirators had done Caesar a great wrong and should pay for it, and that they should revolt against them.

Mark Antony waved Caesar's will before the public. Hearing what Caesar had left to the people would make them

angry with the conspirators, he said, and so he would not read it out. This made the people all the more eager to hear it. But instead of reading out the will, Antony took up Caesar's mantle 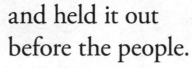 and held it out before the people.

"If you have tears, prepare to shed them now," he said, pointing out the bloodstained holes made by the conspirators as they stabbed Caesar.

"O most bloody sight! Revenge! Kill!" the public began to shout.

"Stay, countrymen,
let me not stir you up to
mutiny," said Antony, putting
the idea of mutiny cleverly
into the people's mind. Then
and only then did he read out
Caesar's will, which explained
that he had left money as
well as part of his gardens
and orchards for public use.

At this the people went wild. They rushed about, saying, "Most noble Caesar! We'll avenge his death! We'll set fire to the houses of those who betrayed him."

Antony did nothing to quieten them, for his very purpose had been to stir up the people against the conspirators.

Octavius Caesar was
Julius Caesar's nephew. He
had been on his way to Rome
with another Roman nobleman
named Lepidus and reached
the city at that very moment.
Antony felt that Octavius had
come at a very fortunate hour.

Chased by an angry mob,
Brutus and Cassius had rushed

out of the city gates.
The people were
now so mad at the
conspirators that they
fell upon an innocent
person and tore him
to pieces just because
his name was Cinna
(the same as one of
the conspirators).

After Caesar's
funeral, Mark Antony,
Octavius Caesar,
and Lepidus formed
a three-member
ruling-group—
the Triumvirate.

Brutus and
Cassius fled to Sardis

in Asia Minor. Staying in
different parts of Sardis, they
began to build a new army.
One evening, Cassius visited
Brutus at his camp and was
shocked to learn that he had
lost his wife. Portia had been
so troubled that she swallowed
poison. Even so, Brutus remained
calm and bravely faced the
challenge of the Triumvirate.

Brutus went on to say that he had learned that Octavius and Antony were arriving with a powerful army, marching toward the plains of Philippi. Brutus wanted their own army to march and meet them at Philippi, but Cassius did not like the idea. However, he agreed when Brutus said that they should not miss this

chance, since they were at the
height of their strength and
now was the time to strike.

After Cassius had left,
Brutus settled down to sleep,
asking his attendant Lucius to
play some music on the harp.
Suddenly, the candlelight
grew dim and a ghostly figure
appeared in the half-darkness—

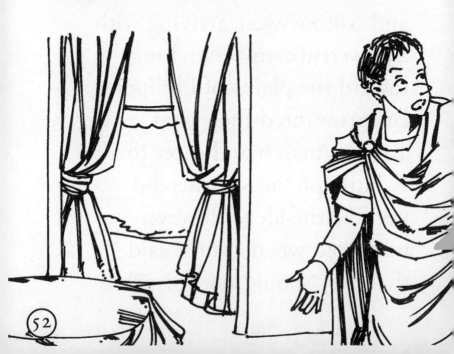

that of Julius Caesar.
Brutus's blood ran cold and
his hair stood on end.

"You will see me at Philippi,"
said Caesar's spirit, and then
vanished. Lucius, however, said

he had not seen a thing. But
Brutus knew that Julius Caesar
had indeed visited him in spirit,
which led him to give marching
orders even earlier than had
been planned with Cassius.

Birds of ill omen—ravens,
crows, and kites—flew above
the army as it marched, until the

two armies met on the plains
of Philippi. Then Brutus and
Cassius bade farewell to each
other in case the battle was lost
and they never met again.

Brutus gave the order
to attack, but he gave it too
early and Antony's soldiers
closed in upon his own.

Cassius, whose eyes were weak, caught sight of his tents burning and sent Titinius to see if the soldiers were friends or foes. Then he sent his attendant, Pindarus, to a hilltop to observe Titinius. Pindarus saw Titinius being made to get down from his horse by soldiers who were

shouting for joy. When he told Cassius, he took it as a sure sign of defeat. He asked Pindarus to kill him with the very sword that Cassius had stabbed Caesar with.

Sadly Pindarus obeyed his master and fell down, crying, "Caesar, you are avenged."

The sun was setting when Titinius came back unhurt. He

had been made to get down
from his horse by Brutus's
soldiers, who had actually

triumphed over Antony. When he discovered that Cassius had died because of an error, Titinius killed himself.

When Brutus arrived and saw the two bodies lying in the red rays of the setting sun, he said, "O Julius Caesar, you are mighty yet. Your spirit walks abroad and turns our swords into

our own bodies." However, he went back to the battlefield and led his soldiers to a second fight.

But this second round went to Mark Antony, and Brutus lost most of his friends and soldiers. Needing to rest, he sat on a rock, tears falling. He asked his

friends and followers to kill him,
as he would rather die than be
captured. "The ghost of Caesar has
appeared before me and I know
my hour has come," he said.

His friends refused and fled
from the scene, as Antony and
Octavius were getting nearer
every minute. There was only one
follower left—Strato. At Brutus's
request, Strato held out Brutus's
sword while Brutus ran toward
it, crying, "Caesar, now be still!"

So when Octavius and
Antony reached the spot,